ALIEN VIGILANTE AIRCRAFT

A FRANK SHANNON STORY

RONALD DEAN DURBIN

ISBN: 978-1-63950-305-6 (sc)
ISBN: 978-1-63950-306-3 (e)

Writers Apex

Gateway Towards Success

8063 MADISON AVE #1252
Indianapolis, IN 46227
+13176596889
www.writersapex.com

March 27, 2020

The last thing Lieutenant Colonel Frank Shannon did was push the eject button. His bird was going down, now in a safe area, but he was too close to the ground. He ejected, but his carriage was dragged on the ground, and it rolled and rolled. Frank never knew any of this. When he hit the ground, the impact knocked him out. His body was shredded. Only the quick response of the rescue chopper saved his life. The Air Force gave up on Frank ever recovering, coming out of his deep coma. Tubes breathed for him. Other tubes fed him. His heart was strong and was working on its own. With this, the Air Force medically retired Frank at the rank of colonel.

Sara had held on for forty-five days, waiting. Frank had lost both legs and broke his left arm. The rest of his body seemed to be okay, but he wasn't waking up. The doctors didn't have a clue why. They told Sara at day one hundred, they would unplug Frank and let him die. Sara couldn't take watching him die. She gave up and filed for divorce. After their son Sean graduated from high school, she headed back home to Albany. This put their twenty-year-old son Kelly as his next of kin. Sara could get half of his retirement, but nothing from his 100 percent disability. Kelly set up a bank account for his medical retirement to go into. After one hundred days in the hospital, the director met with Kelly to talk about unplugging Frank and letting him die.

Beek had been keeping up with Frank's care and was not happy. These earthlings didn't use common sense when it came to their patients. Back home on Zuppo, Frank would have already been released. Beek decided it was time for him to act. Frank's medication was only sedating him. It wasn't treating his brain's issues. Beek inserted the necessary medicine into the IV. It would take a few hours, but Frank would wake up.

Kelly wasn't giving up. He was going to have his father transferred to the hospital's rehab center. No one was unplugging his dad. Kelly came by to tell this to his body.

With a look of astonishment, Kelly saw his father sitting up and drinking coffee. "Dad!"

Frank was surprised by Kelly's reaction. He didn't know that he'd been unconscious for more than one hundred days. "What?"

"You're awake."

Again, Frank didn't know anything about his accident. He woke up and asked for some coffee. "How long was I out?"

Kelly, still looking at him with wide eyes, replied, "Three and a half months."

Frank had no knowledge what was happening or what had happened to him. "Didn't anyone tell you that I woke up?" Actually, the doctors had just removed Frank's tubes. He was drinking his first coffee in months. "How's Mom?" Kelly didn't hesitate to give the bad news to his dad. "I guess you haven't been told, but you're divorced. She's fine though."

Frank couldn't believe it. His wife had left him. Everything was okay before. "Divorced?"

"Yes. She's moved to New York State with her family. I've been making the calls on your care."

This was too much for Frank to handle. Without thinking, he got out of bed and collapsed. With a stupid look on his face, he looked up at Kelly for a hand up. Frank wasn't much help, but they were able to get him into a chair. "Where are my legs?"

Kelly didn't know where to begin. He was not really ready for this conversation. "What do you remember?"

Frank had a blank expression. "Nothing."

"Okay, Dad, you were flying a Raptor when your power shut off. You guided your jet away from a residential area, but when you ejected, you were too close to the ground. Your chute opened, and you hit the ground hard. Your seat rolled a hundred meters. Your legs were ripped off. A nurse passing by was the first person on the scene. She tied off your legs to stop your blood loss. A chopper brought you in. You've been on life support ever since. Just now, the doctors were wanting to unplug you, but I said no. We have exceeded the number of days you can stay here, so I was going to have them move you to a rehab center." Kelly was exasperated. He felt like he was letting his father down. Tears began rolling down Kelly's face. He couldn't believe his father was near death and now they were just talking.

Sitting in a chair, Frank's brain started thinking about what was next. "Okay. I'm awake now, and I can decide what's next. Thanks for all that you've done, Kelly." Frank had lost fifty pounds during his one-hundred-day stay.

Kelly worked at a golf pro shop and attended Georgetown University part-time. Every other day, he would come and visit his dad for a few hours. He was very tired and was ready for Frank to take over his own affairs. "Dad, you look good. I'm really tired. I need to go home and check on things."

Again, Frank was beginning to figure out a course of action. "Thanks. You said I'm single? What about the house and stuff?"

Still not feeling comfortable telling his dad about the breakup, Kelly told him briefly, "It's all locked up. Mom took her stuff. I don't think the Air Force thought you were going to recover. They retired you at the rank of full colonel. Right now, it's a medical retirement, but that won't change."

Frank would be able to go forward from here. "All right. I need to think about a lot of stuff. I'll be in touch. Do I have a phone?"

Kelly hadn't done anything about a phone or the home. He was just thinking about his father's care. "No. It didn't survive the crash. But I'll get you one tomorrow."

Frank saw a very tired son and knew he was ready for some relief. "No. I'll take care of it. Thanks. Go and see your wife." Frank was now totally free to figure out what was next.

Now Frank had to figure out how to get back into his bed. That was the answer. He needed to check out of the hospital and get into his bed at home.

Just then, his answer walked into the room. Leroy was six feet five inches tall and weighed 260 pounds. Recently, he had retired from the Air Force and was working as a medical technician in the hospital. He wasn't happy with his job, but it was a job. "Colonel, what are you doing out of bed?"

"And you are?"

"Leroy, sir. I used to be in the squadron, but I just retired."

"I think I remember seeing you around the hangar."

The colonel was a rising star. He was the squadron commander of an F-22 unit at Langley. Then he crashed. Now he was Leroy's patient. "Come on, sir, let's get you back into bed."

Frank saw a way to get things moving, and Leroy was the answer. "Leroy, could you get a couple of days off?"

"Why, sir?" Leroy had no clue as to what the commander might want.

"I'm going to need some help getting situated back into my home. I'm willing to pay you, say, seven hundred a day for a few days."

"When do I start?"

"You can start by doing what we need to do to get me released."

With that, Leroy gathered the release papers. The staff was not happy that the colonel was leaving without the doctor signing off. Leroy rolled the colonel on out of the hospital and to his car. Leroy drove a yellow Caddy, so he had plenty of room for his passenger.

Frank didn't have any clothes, but he had his watch and wallet. Kelly had left him the keys to his home, so Leroy drove him home. Leroy had borrowed a wheelchair and a couple of masks from the hospital. After Frank crashed, the nation had a pandemic begin. A virus from China was killing people, and it had now reached the United States in full force. Every face had to be covered for now.

Now at home, Frank was wiped out. "Leroy, take a two-hour break, and then we can get going again." Leroy picked

Frank up out of the chair and placed him on his bed. Frank was out like a light.

Later when Leroy returned, he helped get Frank dressed. No legs, but he still wanted his jeans. They were cut and taped for now. Frank wanted to go in his own car, but Leroy refused. "We'll stay in my car."

Google showed Frank where he could get a handicap van. Leroy parked his Caddy on the dealership's lot. Next, they visited AT&T and picked up a new Samsung. He still had the same number and account. Next, they took the van to an electric cart store. Again, Google showed them where. Frank could drive the van if they turned the front driver's seat so Frank could hop in. The van had four captain's chairs, and all swiveled. The gas and brake pedals were located on the steering wheel. For now, Frank drove, heading back to the dealership to pick up Leroy's Caddy and then home to 114 Alamo Court.

Frank would be needing a lot of new gadgets for around the house. Having no legs really complicated life. Reggie from next door saw the strange new van and wondered what was happening. The van door came open, and the lift came out with Frank on for a ride. Reggie just watched in disbelief. Leroy parked his Caddy next to the van.

Next, they created a shopping list, and Frank asked Leroy if he could handle everything. Leroy smiled and took off in his Caddy.

Reggie never said anything. He just followed Frank into the house. "What do you need, Frank?"

"I need some Jack and Coke Zero." Then Frank pointed to where things were, and Reggie poured two. The two men toasted by clicking their glasses and then silently sipped their drinks.

After a bit, Reggie explained, "Sara told us she was going back to New York. Sorry, Frank."

Frank didn't respond. He nodded and just sipped his drink.

The two men sat looking at each other. "I know you don't have legs, but how's the rest of you doing?"

"I need another Jack and Coke before I answer."

Reggie poured Frank another.

Frank had been the squadron commander of the twenty-seventh. He had been picked up or selected to become a full colonel. His next job was to be the deputy commander of the wing. Now he was retired with 100 percent disability. "Reggie, what was is no more. I had a wife and a military career, and they are both gone. I think what is left of me is okay. But tonight, I'll be getting drunk."

With that, Reggie exited. "I'm next door if you need anything."

Leroy had gone to the Kroger down the street and was back soon. Frank had places for everything, and the food items were placed there.

Next, Frank had another drink. "Leroy, let's start tomorrow around noon, okay?"

"Yes, sir." Leroy was out the door and gone.

Frank spoke, but Leroy didn't hear him. "I'm just Frank now. Call me Frank." He would always be the colonel to Leroy.

Leroy and Beek passed each other.

"Hello, Frank."

Frank was surprised by Beek's casual greeting. He had no idea he was talking to an alien from Zuppo. "Who the hell are you? Whatever you're selling, I don't want any, and get out of my home."

Beek just poured himself a drink. He knew where the mixings were. He fixed himself a drink and then just sat down.

Frank couldn't believe his actions and just glared at him.

"Frank, we have some business to talk about, but it can wait until in the morning. Today, you're going to get drunk and forget what we talk about, so I'll just wait."

Frank was now working on his fourth drink and didn't care anymore what Beek did or said.

After his sixth drink, Frank dozed. Beek rolled him into his bedroom and sat him on his bed. He left a small pitcher there for Frank's needs.

In the morning, Beek woke Frank up with a cup of coffee.

"Who the hell are you, and why are you still in my house?"

"To make a long story short, I'm not from this place. I'm going home soon, but I needed to deliver an aircraft to you." Beek handed a photo of Frank's new aircraft. It looked like a smaller version of the B-2, except the wing tips curved up.

"Okay, you've got my attention. We don't have any of these."

"No. It wasn't made here. It was made on my planet, Zuppo."

"It's okay that I don't believe any of this?"

Beek switched to telepathy. "I have been here on earth for a while, and I have been called back home. I don't want to leave this plane with any nation, but I'm willing to leave it with the commander."

"I'm not the commander anymore. I'm retired. I can't fly your aircraft. I don't have any legs."

"To me and Leroy, you will always be the commander. You don't need legs to fly this plane. We are going to need Leroy to move out there with us. He can service the aircraft."

"Out there?"

"Utah. We should take a day and fly out there. I have the plane in a hangar near here."

"You have this plane near here, Washington, DC?"

"The short answer is yes."

"What's the longer answer?"

"Before we go any further, we need to include Leroy. He'll be here around noon."

"I know. I told him."

"I just didn't know how much you would remember. Also, you can't tell anyone else about the plane."

"That's not a problem because I don't believe there is one."

"Don't tell Leroy anything. We can just say we need to pick up a few other things."

"I'm okay with that."

After Leroy showed, everyone got into the van. For now, Beek was going to drive. So they left Alamo Court and took 278 down to I-64 in order to connect with Loop 664 heading south. Pughsville Road led to Grant Street and a small hangar.

"Leroy, what you are about to see is totally top secret. After you've seen it, you can't tell anyone else about it."

Leroy didn't have a clue what Beek was talking about. He just shook his head, thinking, *This man is crazy.*

As they drove up to the small hangar, its doors opened. Beek pulled in. There in the hangar with them was the new fighter jet. "For now, let's call it an F-40."

Frank and Leroy were in disbelief. Next, a ramp opened, and everyone entered the F-40. Frank could drive right up to the front seats. He locked in his cart and hopped into a seat. Without speaking, Beek started backing the jet out of the hangar. Leroy took one of the two remaining seats. Beek taxied the aircraft to the runway. Before taking off, he pushed the cloaking button, and now the aircraft looked like a Cessna. Without much noise, the jet took off and climbed to three thousand feet. Beek hit autopilot and turned to start answering questions.

Leroy started, "What the hell is this?"

"It's one of my planet's jet fighters. It can fly in an atmosphere or in space. I've told the commander that I need to return home and I want to leave this bird with you two. You can fly anywhere you want. It is 100 percent stealth. There will be times that a mission will need to be carried out by a third party with discretion.

"Some of my people are staying. They will contact you with information that could be helpful. Otherwise, you are on your own." After a couple of hours, the jet started its approach. Beek didn't need to do anything. The jet just landed on the ranch's runway and taxied to its hangar. Inside the hangar were two more F-40s.

"Let's take a tour of your ranch."

Leroy asked, "Whose ranch?"

"It will be yours as soon as you agree to move here. But you have a requirement of not ever selling it. We have set aside a nice salary for you and you, too, Commander. When you retire, someone will contact you about the ranch."

The property was adjacent to a government refuge for wild mustangs. No one lived within fifty miles of the ranch houses. "Exactly what you choose to do with the place is up to you. Commander, we have a device similar to a skateboard that you can use to work a garden if you choose. You have exactly matching homes with a fenced-in backyard. There is a barn with a small tractor you can use.

"For the sake of time, let's take a tour with the jet. It has hover capabilities. We are going to need a few days together for you to learn all her possibilities. She has the ability to reverse gravity. We can take off vertically or by using a runway. It can function like a helicopter."

Since they were using it like a chopper, the cloaking device made it appear like a Bell chopper. This part of Utah was very dry, but the ranch had water and the mustangs liked drinking from their little lake. It had canyons and some tall hills. There were a wide variety of trees and cacti.

By now, Frank had grown tired and said as much. They returned to their new furnished homes. "Leroy, Frank and I will meet up with you after his nap."

Leroy nodded and set off to inspect his home. All this was too much for his brain to accept.

Beek and Frank headed to the other new home. Once inside the kitchen, Beek made two drinks. He and Frank toasted. The Jack and Coke Zero took the edge off of Frank's nervousness. Beek showed him the master bedroom and left for Frank to take care of his business. "I'll be in the living room when you wake up, Frank."

Frank was totally wiped out. He didn't answer. He just gave a wave. Inside the home, Frank used a wheelchair. He was getting used to moving around without legs. After the restroom business, it was time to check out the bed. He wondered if this could all really be happening or if he would suddenly wake up.

When Frank awoke, it was to the aroma of onions cooking on the stove. Leroy was back, and he and Beek were cooking supper. After supper, they returned to the DC area.

"Take a couple of days and tell me if you guys are interested in going forward." With that said, Beek exited.

Leroy headed for the Caddy, and Frank had two more drinks before turning in.

In the morning, Frank began to transition to Utah. He notified Kelly and asked him to inform Sean. Frank was taking a consulting job in Utah and would be leaving as soon as possible. "Would you and Jax like to live in this place? If not, I'm going to sell it."

"Sure, Dad. Just let me talk with her about it."

"Here's what I'm thinking. You guys can pay the utility bills and I'll make the house payments."

Next up was Beth and Reggie. They came over for supper. Frank was able to do spaghetti and meatballs. Beth did the salad while Reggie set the table and poured some drinks.

"Okay. Are you ready?"

"Ready for what?"

"What's next. I'm moving to Utah to be a consultant with a company there."

"That was quick."

"Not really. The HR guy was waiting for me to come out of my coma. You ran into him the other day, Reggie." Beth was concerned about the house. "What happens to this place?"

"I've offered it to Kelly. If he doesn't want it, then I'll need to find a trustworthy realtor."

Beth knew Frank was teasing. Beth would be that realtor.

Leroy had a wife and three children. Malcom, twenty-two, was single. Bernice, twenty, had a special friend, Jason. And Charles, eighteen, was also single. Leroy told Frank, "I'm not moving out to Utah right now. If I can work on the aircraft at the local hangar, then I'm interested."

When Beek came by, the information was a yes and a not yet. Beek was okay with both answers. They would begin the process of training both on the qualities of the F-40.

Kelly and Jax decided to take the deal. Kelly hired two friends to help. Next, he rented a van using Frank's credit card and moved. After moving their goods in, they moved the stuff that Frank was taking out to Utah. Next, the van pulled Frank's van on a carrier, and he and Kelly headed to Utah and Tooele County. Kelly was given Frank's car. Sean had come by from Albany to tell his dad hello and help with the move. Now Sean was wondering about jobs in Utah.

Leroy was having a little trouble convincing his wife that Utah was a good place to retire at. She was not leaving this home. This was her retirement home. So Leroy told Beek he could not take the job. He was willing to train a newbie. Beek thanked Leroy for his help to this point and asked if he would consider working three days a week and live in the DC area. Leroy agreed. Frank was okay with Sean getting involved in the corporation. Sean was offered the second home in Utah and jumped on it.

While Sean drove his Dodge out to Utah, Beek met with Frank. "We have a situation."

"What does that mean?"

"That means your training is going live. I, we, need to take out eight silos in Iran. They have ballistic missiles that are ready to launch. They will probably be heading to Israel."

"Go on."

"An ICBM (intercontinental ballistic missile) plant has completed work on a dozen missiles. These are not defensive weapons. You know ICBMs are for attacking. They also have nuclear capabilities. They have placed eight in their silos."

Frank was caught off guard. "So I'm just supposed to trust you and go and blow up stuff?"

Beek was through being polite. "No, you can stay here, but I'm going."

Frank wasn't sure that he wanted to go, but he would. "Okay. Just checking. I'll go. Just the two of us this trip, okay?"

Now Beek needed to do some quick on-the-job training (OJT). "First, Frank, you need to get into flight clothes.

Next, we have meals ready to eat (MREs). The plane has water and oxygen. So we can leave as soon as you change clothes."

Frank had six-inch legs now. Beek had five flight suits made for him. "You will want to wear a T-shirt and then this."

Beek handed Frank a shirt that looked like it was made out of fish scales. "Okay, this is a little different."

Beek knew Frank had never seen anything like it before. "This will replace a few things. You don't need a girdle any longer. When you pull Gs, it will tighten. If you eject, it will tighten and protect your neck from whiplash."

Frank was not surprised. He just put on his new shirt. He didn't have shoes, so he was ready.

Frank and Beek entered the F-40 starship. This one he named after his ex-wife, Sara. They had two more, so when he spoke about *Sara*, he was talking about number 1. Frank drove up to his seat. It could rotate 360 degrees. He reversed it and hopped in. Straps were fastened, and the ship left the hangar.

The lessons for right now were over. The console was all digital. Beek began pushing the screen. Frank felt his scale shirt stiffen, and a second later, polarities were reversed and the ship shot upward. Afterburners were ignited, and they shot into the night on April 3. Frank never got used to the Gs. He just gritted his teeth and tried to breath.

Some sixty years earlier, the SR-71 Blackbird used to launch to the edge of space. Beek had been one of the consulting engineers who designed the Blackbird. The Department of Defense folks didn't like the design of the F-40, but most of the components were the same. The Blackbird went so fast that the air acted like sandpaper on its paint. Paint had to be built into the metal. As we journeyed to the moon, we were already using space suits from the Blackbird. The F-40 didn't need space suits. The cockpit was pressurized. Frank and Beek did wear helmets with oxygen just to be safe. With afterburners, they used some of their jet fuel. When flying at a regular speed, the jet converted regular air into fuel by concentrating and burning it. Beek put on the stealth mode as well as the hologram of an Israeli F-35. Now at the edge of space, they sped on to their mission.

Before blowing up some silos, they would need to refuel. Next, Beek prepared for midair refueling. He had a NATO code and switched the hologram to a British F-35 for the refueling. Israel always refueled NATO aircraft with no questions asked. Now just past midnight with full tanks, Beek broke away and thanked the Israeli refueler. Next, Beek showed Frank how to lock in GPS coordinates. "Iran, here we come."

The hologram switched back to the Israeli F-35. Radar would not pick them up, but just in case of a visual sighting, they would look like an Israeli F-35.

Time wise, the trip was short. Beek soon had his targets and let his satellite-directed weapons drop down to the silos. The satellites would forward video of the results. Beek didn't want to stay around and be detected. They went back up to orbit and headed back to Washington.

The satellite footage was amazingly clear. The silos were destroyed along with their contents. Those ICBMs would do no damage.

Frank's head was trying to take in all that had just happened. He just flew, undetected, into another country and blew up some of their assets.

Iran had been a good friend of the United States before the Shah died. Overnight, life changed. Their embassy was attacked and captured. The workers there were now prisoners of a radical group. They used religion to gain control of a country. Iran began reaching out to others who wanted to gain control of the country they lived in. Iran showed them. Now they had agents and followers in several countries. The country was growing influence all over the Middle East.

Now up in orbit, Beek began with his lessons again. He showed Frank how to connect with the video of the attack. The smart weapons used lasers instead of conventional explosives. All eight silos went up in smoke.

The speed of the Blackbird was kept top secret. The speed of *Sara* was even faster. Soon, they descended back down to Washington and home.

Beek showed Frank his watch. Alarms had gone off at the hangar. Someone was there waiting for them. Beek went to plan D. He called Senator David Dodd—also from Zuppo. The senator was on the Armed Services Committee. He put in a call to the secretary of the Air Force, Sharon Alexander. She would check into it.

The F-40 did a vertical landing and moved into the hangar. Frank was still shaking his head as he got back onto his electric carrier. During descent, his scale shirt tightened and then relaxed as they landed. Still, he was ready to get it off.

Beek warned him that some things were about to happen and he should do just as Beek directed. "When I say move, we have to move. Okay?"

As they exited the aircraft, twenty rifles were pointed at them. "Freeze. Don't move."

Another voice said, "You are on Department of Defense property. Don't move or we will be forced to shoot."

Then Frank heard a cell phone ring. Brigadier General Wirst answered her phone. "Hello, Teresa. Put me on speaker. This is your boss, Sharon Alexander." Brigadier General Wirst followed her orders and put the cell on speaker. "Beek and Colonel, you two should leave at this time."

Brigadier General Wirst was outraged. "They can't leave. I've put them under arrest."

"Teresa, stand down." Sharon Alexander had not been secretary of the Air Force for very long, but she knew she was in charge.

Beek spoke, "Let's go." Frank was startled but began moving.

Rifles still pointed at them, they slowly moved away and kept going.

Meanwhile, Brigadier General Wirst said, "Madam Secretary, these two are breaking several laws by landing here."

"Who am I?"

"You are the secretary of the Air Force."

"That makes me your boss. Follow my orders here and now or be reassigned to Alaska as a squadron commander."

Beek pushed another button, and *Sara* lifted off and would return in one hour to take Frank back to Utah.

"Madam Secretary, these two just landed a strange aircraft at a Defense Department hangar. I've placed them under arrest."

"Teresa, who is the security forces officer with you?" Lieutenant Johnson answered for himself, "Madam Secretary, this is Lieutenant Johnson. How can I help you?"

"Lieutenant, stand down. Next, you and your people get on your Chinook and go back to JB Langley-Eustis. Take the general with you."

"Yes, ma'am."

"Any questions, Teresa?"

"All is clear. But what about this jet?" Teresa would get to the bottom of this back at the base.

"Teresa, what jet are you talking about?"

As she looked around, the jet was gone. Stunned, Teresa could say nothing.

Beek's phone rang. "Hello. Yes, ma'am. Sharon wants you to stop by her office before you go home."

Frank was surprised. "She wants to see me?"

When he got to the gate at the Pentagon, he was given a VIP parking sticker. Next, he found his spot and went in to visit with Sharon Alexander, the secretary of the Air Force.

There to greet him was Leroy Brown in uniform, wearing the rank of chief master sergeant. "Sir, we've been promoted."

CNN was conducting a press conference with the director of Foreign Affairs for Israel. "So you're saying it was not an Israeli jet that blew up Iran's silos?"

"I can't say it any clearer than that."

Al Jazeera was having a profit day by saying an Israeli jet was seen in the area. They didn't care if it was true. They were just counting the dollars coming in by saying an Israeli jet was seen not long before things blew.

BBC was broadcasting that no one was taking credit for it.

———◦◦◦◦◦———

"Hello, Frank."

"Hello, Madam Secretary."

"In here, just call me Sharon."

"You're the boss."

"Yes. I still am. Frank, we've brought you back onto active duty."

"Is that possible?"

"You were medically retired. It wasn't that hard. What was more difficult was the two-star promotion."

Frank just sat there. He couldn't believe his ears. "Now I know that's not possible."

"Frank, the president knows what you were doing last night with Beek. Also, you've been awarded the Congressional Medal of Honor. You guided your Raptor away from civilians at the risk of your life. He'll need to pin this on you later next week. I pushed through your promotion by making you my aide."

Frank was just stunned by all that was going on. He just sat there.

"You will be connected with Homeland Security. Your new rank is major general. That will give you a lot of sway.

"But I have more. Your son Sean is ready to start college. I'd like him to go to the Air Force Academy. He'll need to be there on the first of August.

"Kelly can't go because he's already married. But I can give him a full scholarship through the ROTC program. That means he would have to serve in the military for four years. He'll be paid as a staff sergeant. We need to get them cracking."

Still stunned by all that was happening, Frank just sat there.

"My secretary will give you your promotion orders as you leave. I know you have uniforms, but we need you to get your rank changed. Get back with me after you speak with your sons. You can go."

Frank didn't snap too. He just spun his cart around and rolled out.

On the way through the outer office, he was handed a bunch of stars: one set for his blues, another set for his flight suit, and still another set for his BDUs.

Leroy met him at the door. "Sir, now I'm officially your aide. I can get all the rank you are missing and get them put on your clothes."

It took maybe two hours, but finally, Teresa returned to her office. Her name was no longer on the door. Lieutenant Johnson was standing next to the door. "Ma'am, you can't go in there."

"Certainly, I can. This is my office."

Lieutenant Johnson was trying to be respectful, but Teresa was making it difficult. "Not anymore."

Teresa opened the door to find her deputy sitting at her desk. "Kory, what are you doing here?"

Kory Miles had been the deputy commander under Brigadier General Wirst. Now, today, he had been promoted to become the new commander with the promotion to brigadier general. It wasn't official yet, but the secretary of the Air Force frocked him and he was wearing his one star.

"Hello. I'm here because this is now my office. I'm told you were fired."

"Ma'am, I need you to leave this building. If you don't, then I will cuff you and drop you off at the main gate."

Teresa had never been spoken to like this before. "What the hell is going on here?"

"You've been fired for disobeying a direct order from the secretary of the Air Force. She also told me to have my butt in this chair within the hour or she'd find another colonel who would. Just leave quietly."

Stunned, Teresa left quietly.

Both sons were interested in flying the F-40. Going to college was an added benefit. Both accepted the offers from the secretary of the Air Force.

Now the second house was not going to be used by anyone. Kelly would stay in Frank's home in DC until school started in the fall. Sean would be moving to Colorado Springs, Colorado. Leroy would be staying in his home in DC as well.

Frank needed to go by the Military Personnel Flight office. His records needed to be changed, and he also needed a two-star sticker for his windshield and a new ID card because of his rank change. Now Leroy was officially working for him, so he could get a lot of his errands run.

He went back to the hangar to see if *Sara* had returned. She had, and so they flew home. Frank could not remember being so tired. There was no Beek, so Frank typed in Home, and *Sara* flew home.

Frank's training with Beek was going great. Time was flying by. Today, the fourteenth of April, Frank found himself in the Rose Garden of the White House. Suddenly the president's music was introducing his arrival. Everyone stood, except Frank. With this, he became furious. He needed to rise when the commander came into the room. He accepted the fact that his wife jumped ship. He had accepted the fact that his military career was over. He had accepted the fact that he had lost his legs, but he could not accept sitting when the president entered. Now he was trembling with anger.

The president, Teddy Jones, noticed and told him not to be nervous. It would be over in a few moments. For Frank, it would not be over until he could rise when the president entered. That would mean a trip to Walter Reed Medical Center and their prosthetic department. The next time, he would be able to rise.

Teddy Jones had some nice words to say about Frank and then pinned on the Congressional Medal of Honor. Both sons were present and proud of their father. And then it was over. There was a reception inside the White House. Frank looked terrific in his blue Class As.

Chief Brown was there, and Frank told him to get him an appointment at the medical center. There was a "Yes, sir." Frank began to calm down after that simple conversation.

With Frank's new rank, his new legs became a high priority at the hospital. Also, President Jones had phoned to check on the legs. They were made, and Frank could now stand. His flight training with *Sara* was continuing. His sons were doing flight ground school together at the Leesburg airport. Soon, Kelly would head to the AFROTC summer camp at Lackland in San Antonio. Chief Brown was enjoying his new rank and job. Days turned into weeks as the summer passed.

Soon, August arrived, and Sean reported to the Air Force Academy at Colorado Springs. Kelly was set up to attend Georgetown University on a full-time basis.

There were two trouble spots that would concern Frank and the US. The Kyrgyz were being attacked by the Tajis. Under Soviet rule, there was no problem with the border. Afterward, the Tajis wanted more. Families were moved out by the Tajis, and fighting started. The United Nations got the fighting stopped, but no one knew for how long.

The other hot spot was Hamas digging tunnels into Egypt in order to smuggle people and contraband in and out. Frank got a call from the prime minister of Israel. "Good morning, General."

"Good morning, sir."

"So you know who this is?"

"Your secretary said you would be calling. How can I help you?"

"Directly to the point, I need some tunnels blown that Hamas is using to bring contraband into Gaza."

"Why are you calling me?"

"We are both friends with Beek."

"Why not just call him?"

"I did. He said it's your call now. He said something about retiring."

"I need those tunnels blown. Lives are at stake. If we do it, there will be fighting back. If you do it, they won't know who to fight with."

"I would need photos, evidence."

"No problem. Where are you today?"

"I'm in Utah."

"It's on its way."

On November 11, 2020, Frank went out to check the mailbox, and there was Beek. "Hello. What's up?"

Beek had just put a package into Frank's box. "Nothing, actually. I live next door now. I'm retired."

"I don't understand."

"I'm not going back. I'll spend whatever time I have left here. This property was open, so I took it."

"I still don't understand."

"Beek is a rank. It would be like your field marshal. From now on, I'm just Adam Green. Soon I' ll switch it to Glen Adams. Adam Green has been around too long."

"Wow. When did you get to earth?"

"My ship arrived on September 2, 1949. Things were still settling down after what you call World War II. Twenty-five came with me on that visit. It takes two years of travel time. We were in a hypersleep for most of that time. I don't want to do that again, so I'm just going to stay here."

Frank had a package in his mailbox. "Mind if I go and open this?"

"No, go ahead." So they parted for now.

Frank knew what the package was and tried not to act excited. Frank opened the small package. Inside were two thumb drives. He inserted the first one. This actually showed a video of people moving big boxes on tracks like a train. The second thumb drive showed the location of three of the tunnels. These would be his targets. He would do it today.

Next door, Beek answered, "Yes, how may I help you?"

"I need some weapon's assistance."

So they talked. There in the hangar, they had some bombs that could go into the ground for about ten feet and then explode. This is what they decided to take with them.

Chief Brown had *Sara* ready to go after just one hour. Beek was ready and stopped by to check on Frank.

Frank was wearing his new scale shirt. "I'm ready. We should drop the chief off in DC."

So everything was loaded, including one Chief Brown. The flight to Washington took almost two hours. The hologram was that of a Cessna. They dropped off the chief and headed toward the Middle East. Now the aircraft looked like a British F-35. Once again, refueling over Israel.

Frank then took over the con (controls). He plugged in his thumb drive and pulled up the coordinates. Today, they would blow up three tunnels.

On the ground, or should I say just leaving tunnel, Fox-three was the last of seven thousand rockets. Today, they were all in pieces, but soon Israel would feel the burning and suffering that was due them. The workers were on a high. Israel had done everything in its power to stop them, but now Israel would pay.

Almost all the rocket parts were out of the tunnel when the firestorm hit. Fire flew out both ends of the tunnel or cave. At each end, flames shot out and up. All inside were now martyrs. The high from seconds ago was now gone. No words were spoken; just tears came. The trucks pulled away heading toward their assembly plant.

The Israeli satellites picked up the three flames shooting out from the tunnels. The mission had been a success. Frank and Beek went back up to twelve thousand feet and headed for home.

On the ground, Akeem was notified that a British F-35 had been spotted moments before the explosions. On that day, he lost thirty-five men, and another thirty-five were wounded. He wrote down, "Kill seventy Brits."

Frank pushed the Return Home button, and *Sara* flew right into their hangar. "Thanks for your help, Beek. Now I need to sleep."

With only a wave, Beek headed to his home. Frank headed to his bed. And he turned off his phone.

Frank had gone to sleep around 0400. So when Beek stopped by, he was still sleeping. Beek had brought him some coffee from next door. Frank was not expecting a visit so early in the morning. "What's up?"

"I have a follow-up visit with Dr. Best. Can I get you to ride along?"

Frank was surprised. "Sure. When?"

"We need to leave in about one hour."

"What's going on, Beek?"

Beek was almost in tears. "Beek is not my name. It 's my rank. People can't be friends with me because I'm the boss. To you, I'm just Beek. Today, I'm Adam Green. Soon, I'll become Glen Adams."

At Dr. Best's office, Beek was shown in to a private counseling area. Dr. Best asked about Frank, "Are you from Zuppo also?"

"No, he's a friend. We'll count him as my next of kin. From my home planet, everyone here is working for me. They would find it hard to be my friend."

"Okay. Well, you have a large mass in your stomach area. It's probably stage 4. We need to go in there and get it out ASAP."

"When?"

"I've scheduled you in for this afternoon."

Beek looked over at a very surprised Frank. "I would like you to join us in the operating room. You'll see me opened up. We have some differences."

Frank did not know what to say. "Uh, yeah, okay, I guess."

"Dr. Best, can you help him get his robe and mask on?"

"Nurse Johnston, can you get the general ready to watch surgery?"

"Of course, doctor. General, follow me."

Frank had never been called by his rank before. It sounded kind of nice. He rolled along behind the nurse.

Meanwhile, Beek was also being prepared but for surgery. Part of that was a living will—who his next of kin was for notification purposes. Frank was going to be his next of kin.

In the operating room, Frank was standing next to Beek. He reached out and took Frank's hand and then spoke to Dr. Best, "Okay. I'm ready now."

Like that, Frank had a new family member. His eyes watered a little. And then it began. First, a mask went over Beek's face, and magic gas began to flow. Beek's eyes closed, and then Dr. Best began. Just below the breastplate, he inserted his scalpel. From there, he cut downward toward his navel.

There was the evil mass. It was as big as a volleyball. It was connected by three strands. The mass came out easily. Now a large whole was there. Dr. Best pointed out his kidneys. "Yours probably have two chambers. Beek's has four. Notice his heart. It has three chambers—one for the lungs, one for the upper body, and one for the lower extremities."

Dr. Della Steet closed up the cavity. Next, Beek was moved to Recovery. Frank stayed with him the whole time, holding his hand. After two and a half hours, they were ready to take Beek to his room at the clinic. That night, Frank slept in a chair next to the bed, holding the hand of his newest family member.

In the outside world, Hamas was fighting mad. They just didn't know who to be mad at. Israel was denying any claim to the bombings but was praising those who had blown the tunnels.

CNN interviewed the prime minister, "Mr. Gandle, are you saying Israel had nothing to do with the blowing up of these tunnels?"

"Absolutely, but we are thankful for whoever did it. Why are these tunnels there? They are there to bring in contraband and illegal people. The only ones unhappy are those breaking the law."

BBC reported, "While no one is claiming responsibility, Israel is very happy that it happened. Egypt is angry with Hamas. But no one has claimed they did it yet."

Al Jazeera claimed that a British F-35 was seen minutes before the explosions happened.

CBS said, "We have confirmations that a British F-35 was seen moments before the explosions, but the prime minister denies they were involved with the blowing of the tunnels."

On the morning of the third day, Beek woke up. Looking around, he saw a sleeping Frank on the sofa. He clicked his remote, and a voice came back. "Mr. Green, are you awake now?"

"Yes. Can I get some coffee? Actually, I'd like two cups."

The new commander, Beek, had chosen his earthly name, Julius Jones. The new Beek had seen off the Zuppos heading home and wished them well. Their journey would last two years. They would sleep for one hundred days and then be sort of awake. After two weeks, they would sleep another one hundred days and so on. But at the end, they would be home.

The new Beek sought out the old, Adam. "Why are you staying here, my friend?"

"I've just had a big ball of cancer cut out of me. Here they call it stage 4. That means that it has already spread. I have only a few months to live."

Julius responded, "I'm truly sorry. But I'll need you to not interfere with my work here." With that, Julius left.

Frank was ready to go home and sleep in his own bed. "Do you mind if I hit the road? I want to take care of a few things, including sleeping in my own bed." Frank hadn't liked the tone of the new Beek's voice. It had almost been a challenge. Adam thought nothing of it.

After two more days, Adam was released to the care of his newest family member. Adam was mobile. Getting "home" was good. But for Adam, home was really two years away—a long ship ride that he would not have survived.

On November 21, Frank and Adam went to get the staples removed from his torso. As the staples came out, tape was placed onto the cut. After two weeks, the tape would start coming off on its own. No baths, just showers. The outside looked pretty good, but the inside was still painful.

Starting on the thirtieth of November, they began traveling together to his chemo appointments. He would not be cured, but his time here could be extended. Adam was scheduled for sixteen chemo appointments. After that, they would play it by ear. Without the chemo, Adam would only last about three months.

All the while, the rest of the world was focusing on Hamas. A bomb had exploded at the central train station in London, leaving hundreds dead and many others wounded.

CNN: "Mike Shantz reporting here in Gaza. The Hamas leader, Akeem, denied any involvement in the bombing but commented on the needless pain of the innocents."

Al Jazeera: "How does it feel to see your people murdered, Europe?"

The White House stated, "We will find out who did this, and they will pay."

The British prime minister said, "The animals who did this will not be able to hide from us."

———∞◦❖◦∞———

Christmas break came and went. The boys visited both Mom and Dad. Airfare was cheap. It was by Dad. Sharon Alexander called on Frank from time to time to make it appear as though he really were working for the Sec-AF.

On January 7, Julius came by to visit Adam in his home. "I have sold this ranch. You and General Shannon need to be gone in one week."

Calmly Adam replied, "That's totally impossible."

"I know I didn't tell you ahead of time, but I don't need to."

"No. You haven't sold this place because it's in General Shannon's name. I gave it to him along with the aircraft."

"You are insane. This place is fifty square miles. Those aircraft didn't belong to you."

"I came with a different set of orders than you. We started with only the aircraft. I built the company up to its current level. I notified the board of directors of my moves all along the way. This place and these aircraft belong to Frank Shannon. Remember, I outrank you. You have to go along with it."

"You outrank me as long as you are alive. You told me that would be just a few months." Then Julius stormed out.

———∞∘▪◈▪∘∞———

On February 1, Sharon Alexander arrived via her own jet. She had called Adam but didn't tell him what the meeting was about. Frank and Adam drove out to the runway to pick her up. Her pilot stayed with the jet. "Hello, guys. Plan A was to have Frank take your three aircraft. Plan B was to make him my aide and put his boys in school full-time. We need to go to plan C."

Frank was surprised. "What is plan C?"

"Senator Dodd has been fired because he would not work with the new Beek, Julius. I need to assign your boys to the CIA full-time, except they'll be working with their father. I can give them the rank of lieutenant. They'll be officially assigned to Homeland Security. While I was at it, I got you one more star, Frank."

Stunned, Frank replied, "You don't mess around."

"The president is working with us on this. I don't like to waste my favors. If we are going to promote your boys, why not get you another star?"

"I'm okay with that."

She went on to explain why the boys were dropping out of school and getting commissioned. "Frank, you are now their full-time teacher, instructor."

Again, Frank was caught off guard. "I'm not ready to do that."

"Who better?"

Adam had been listening, but now he spoke up. "Frank, you are the only one who can."

The secretary of the Air Force wasn't finished with surprises. "Frank, Julius wants your aircraft. I recommend we move them to Area 51 in Nevada. I'll provide you with a Learjet, T-1. You can keep it with you wherever you go. You'll have to fly it to Area 51 to pick up *Sara*."

Frank's life just got a little bit busier. He was an instructor pilot three days a week, and one day a week, he drove Adam to his chemo appointments. Frank gave permission to his two sons to tell one person only what they were up to. Sean told his mother, and Kelly told his wife.

Lt. Gen. Frank Shannon lived in Utah with his son Sean. They would fly to Area 51 and then into DC and pick up Kelly. For three days, they would all sleep at 114 Alamo

Court. Then Frank and Sean would fly back out to Area 51 and pick up the Learjet.

Back in Utah, Sean was online and studying with the academy. Frank was taking care of his older brother, Adam Shannon. Days became weeks; and weeks, months. It takes a pilot seven years to really become good at it. Time going by without incidents was good.

Residing in Adam's DC apartment, Julius called for a status-update meeting with his generals. In Zuppo, they did not have this rank; but on earth it would be beneficial if their ranks were high. Julius had three commanders with the US equivalent rank of 0-10 or full general. They each had two subcommanders with a rank of 0-8, major general.

The new Beek, Julius Jones, was not waiting for the old Beek to die. He was pressing on with his plans to build an empire. Julius chose a one-hundred-square-mile sandbox, Western Sahara. Two thousand years ago, it had been a garden. Now the desert had moved in, and it was only sand. It had been claimed by many before now, but now only Morocco wanted it. All the while, the Berbers had been living in the sand and just getting by. Some were interested in fighting, but most just wanted to live in peace.

Julius was interested in those who wanted to fight. He had sent General Givens to find and meet with these. (All from Zuppo had chosen American-sounding names upon arrival.) "Bert, how did your trip go?"

"Finding them and talking with someone in authority was difficult. I promised them everything they might ever have dreamed of, and they agreed that we could fight for them."

"Good. We needed their name support."

General Hopkins had gone to China to get a thousand uniforms made. "David, how did your China visit go?"

"They agreed to make the uniforms if we paid them now, and we did."

General Bartle was assigned to speak with Russia. "How did your visit go with Mr. Yutinovic?"

"I asked that he deliver two hundred tanks to the southern portion of Western Sahara. He said, 'Show me the money.' I did, and he agreed to deliver the tanks. The small arms needed to be paid for in advance as well."

The meeting continued for two days as Julius laid down his plan of attack.

Hamas was building five thousand rockets to send to Israel. Israel would respond quickly, killing thousands of Palestinians. The martyrs would die for a reason. The reason is self-rule and official statehood.

—∞∘{◉}∘∞—

The prime minister of Morocco, Delatiff Mousha, had been given $5 million to move slowly to any issue in Western Sahara. The prime minister of Algeria, Ahmed Alotaibe, was willing for his troops to work with Julius in taking over the government of Western Sahara. Algeria already had some men there and would send more as needed. Julius had no intentions of honoring any of his agreements.

—∞∘{◉}∘∞—

May rolled around, and Adam was still here. He was very weak and never got out of bed. His life on earth was almost over. He had no update on Julius and was worried. Just that morning, Hamas started shooting rockets into all parts of Israel. Over the next week, Hamas sent five thousand rockets into all parts of Israel.

On day seven, Israel responded. They dropped leaflets on the Hamas headquarters. "If you want to live, leave this building now. In three hours, we will destroy it." Several hundreds left the building, and three hours later, it was leveled.

Most of the rockets sent by Hamas were blown up in the air. Only a few actually hit the ground. A few hundred Israelis were killed or injured. Hamas lost its headquarters. A few hundred Palestinians were injured, but nothing like what Akeem had hoped.

With the world watching Israel and Hamas, Julius attacked. There were a few outposts that fell. Then he moved against some larger targets. General Givens and his Berber troops moved without opposition. It was all too easy. Julius was laughing to himself.

In Rabat, Morocco, the prime minister was telling the king not to worry about the rebels. The king was uncomfortable but did nothing at this time.

The United Nations was watching, but this had happened before. Time would tell if it were successful.

Senator Dodd flew to Utah and Adam. "Julius is moving to take over Western Sahara. He's working with the Berbers and the Algerians. Right now, they are only in the South.

Bir Gandus and Zug are under his control. He's a few days away from Baggar."

"David, have one of your people contact Julius and tell him that if he will come here in person, I will sign over Zuppo Inc. to him."

"You can't be serious."

"Do it." Adam didn't spend any more energy talking. His life was running on borrowed time and borrowed energy. He needed one last meeting with Julius.

Frank never thought he would see the day when Adam would turn over the company to Julius. It wasn't Frank's decision, and he had to let it go.

David Dodd left to carry out Adam's orders. This was the first time that David had disagreed with Adam. It took all he had to carry out Adam's orders.

There were no more cancer chemo treatments. Frank kept his schedule with his sons. They were flying as well as learning how to drop bombs. The F-40s could fire tank-piercing rounds as well as dropping bombs.

Adam knew his time here was getting shorter. He told Frank as much. "Do you think I could borrow your nine mil? I'm bored, and it will give me something to do if I just clean and load it."

Julius couldn't believe the news about getting the Zuppo company. General Givens could carry on the war against nobody. So Julius flew to Utah. Soon he would recover his aircraft as well.

General Givens pressed on against light resistance. Baggar fell to his troops. Not one tank had been lost. Soon Western Sahara would belong to Julius. Bu Craa was next and then on to the capital, Laayoune. Bu Craa could help finance his new empire. There were large deposits of phosphate waiting to be sold.

The former Spanish Foreign Legion post at Al-Dakhla offered the most resistance thus far, but it fell quickly. General Givens was moving faster than his support could follow. He stopped and allowed everyone two days of rest.

The Berber elders saw the charge north and were not happy. They just wanted to be left alone. They wanted to take care of their families and livestock. The younger Berbers sought power. Sometimes that power can come with a big shock.

Without speaking with the prime minister, King Abdulla ordered two thousand Moroccan soldiers to Laayoune. It would take three days to make it happen, but it would happen. They would arrive on the thirty-first. The thing about aircraft was that they could fly. All working aircraft had already been evacuated north.

———⋄⋄⋄❖⋄⋄⋄———

Adam was so weak; he was almost afraid to go to sleep. He would have a surprise for Julius. The papers transferring ownership of the company had been typed up and were ready for signatures.

David Dodd brought Julius and a subcommander, Roger Curry, in to meet with Adam. Papers were lying on a little table next to Adam's bed. Soon, Julius could start spending the $48 billion he was offered for Zuppo Inc. "I want to thank you for this day, Adam."

From under his hip, Adam pulled out the nine mil. He shot Julius four times before Julius fell. Roger was in a state of shock. "What have you done?"

With a wave of the nine mil, Adam told Roger, "Get out and get out of Africa. I'm making David the new Beek." With that, Roger ran out of the house to his waiting aircraft.

David Dodd couldn't believe that Adam killed Julius. "What have you done?"

"I've just killed a cockroach. Now we'll put you in charge of the company. You'll need to leave the senate. Can you send in Frank?"

"Sure."

Frank came in and saw Julius. "So you wanted to clean my nine mil?"

"I don't have much time left. You couldn't do it, but I could. You can, however, go and blow up some tanks."

"Okay. I'll take the boys along, but we'll just take *Sara*."

"Let the Moroccans know you are coming to blow up some tanks, and they will fill you back up with fuel." Frank asked David to notify King Abdulla that the F-40 would be there soon to blow up some tanks. David also found out that the king was sending a squadron of his F-16s to do the same thing. Two hundred tanks would soon be out of action. General Givens had no air support. It would take Frank twenty-four hours to do all the preparations. They would fly to Morocco and Western Sahara on the thirty-first of May 2021.

On May 30, General Givens was approaching Laayoune. Once inside the city, no one would be able to drive them out without killing a lot of civilians. One more day and they would begin their assault.

Frank and his sons left Utah and headed straight up. They traveled to the edge of earth's atmosphere. Sean had the con. Frank was his copilot. Kelly was checking the weapon's system. Sean used the Israeli hologram of an F-35.

On his radio, Frank got a surprise message from Colonel Gordon Abel. "Good morning, General. We have been instructed to accompany you to Western Sahara for a turkey shoot."

"Sure. Give the prime minister my thanks. I'll just need to refuel, and we can be on our way."

"General, there will be some friendly Moroccan F-16s joining us for the shoot. All are friendly. And yes, we like your image of our aircraft."

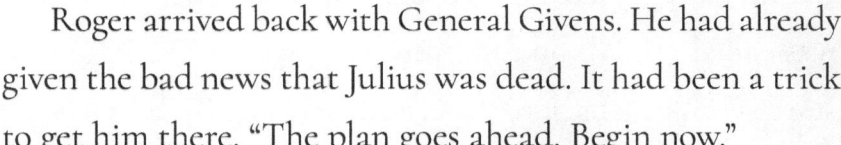

Roger arrived back with General Givens. He had already given the bad news that Julius was dead. It had been a trick to get him there. "The plan goes ahead. Begin now."

With that command, newly promoted General Curry began firing at the military compound just inside the city gates. Laayoune would never be the same. The old colonial capital was under siege. Outside the city gates, the air base was being blasted by General Hopkins.

From the air, Colonel Aladdin Almouie directed Frank to take out the tanks attacking the air base, and the Moroccan jets would focus on the city.

In Gaza, the Israeli aircraft dropped leaflets to the citizens telling them what buildings would be destroyed. If they wanted to stay alive, they should get away from them. Here, there were no innocents. All two hundred tanks would be destroyed.

Frank and the three Israeli jets focused on the tanks attacking the air base. After half of them were destroyed, the others started pulling away. It was too late for the tanks.

Laayoune was damaged, but it would recover. The army base inside the city gates sustained some damage, but not much. The Moroccan jets were successful in killing all the attacking tanks. With night approaching, the attack was called off. All on foot were not shot at. The Algerians started walking back to Algeria. The young Berbers headed to their villages.

That night, two thousand soldiers arrived at the air base and began to restore order. The next morning, squads were sent out to make sure no unfriendly soldiers were still in the area.

Frank and the Israelis returned home. Other Moroccan squads were sent out to the captured cities to make sure everything returned to the preinvasion point. Life was not normal, but it would return to normal.

The issues with Hamas had covered the beginning of the invasion, but the lack of air support cost General Givens. General Givens and his men disappeared. They had been in the desert, now without any support.

ALIEN VIGILANTE AIRCRAFT

CHAPTER 2

A FRANK SHANNON STORY

FOREWORD

This is a work of fiction.
Beyond a few historical facts, this
story came from within me.

With the Secretary of Defense stepping down, President Jones needed a friendly face there. The answer was Sharon Alexander. She had served him well as Secretary of the Air Force. And, she would bring along her general, Frank Shannon. Frank would become Chief of the Joint Chiefs, now, with four stars.

Frank's recovery from his coma had been because of Beek. Beek had been a visiting general from the planet Zuppo. His earthly name had been Adam Green. With no family here on earth, he changed his name to Shannon and became Frank's brother. Beek was set to go back to Zuppo when it was determined that he had stage 4 cancer and would not survive the trip.

His replacement, Julius, came with his own agenda. Julius wanted to set up his own empire. He had set his sites on Western Sahara as his starting point. From there, he would have moved on across the northern part of Africa. The problem was that he needed the aircraft Adam had signed over to Frank for his use as a vigilante. Adam refused to let Julius have the aircraft or to use the company he had set up. Julius proceeded without them. At this point, Adam took out Julius with four rounds from Frank's 9-mil.

The next day, Adam Shannon died as a result of his cancer. Frank had gone back in to pick up his 9-Mil, but Adam was gone. Frank had a local funeral home come and take Adam's body and prepare it for burial there on the estate.

Four days later, Adam Shannon was laid to rest on the ranch. His stone simply read: Arrived on September 2, 1949 and departed on June 2, 2021.

Frank, his sons, some Israeli F-35s, and some Moroccan F-16s took care of the Western Sahara invaders. Most of the newly purchased Russian tanks lay enroute to Algeria. All of those on foot, were allowed to walk east to Algeria.

Back in Gaza, Ahkeem had hoped for all-out-war against Hamas, but the Israelis only hit selected targets with only a few civilian losses.

Prime Minister, Joshua Gandle, called Frank again to ask for his help. His Mossad had two unmarked F-35s and needed one more for a short mission. Frank said he couldn't go, but Sean could help out. "Fax me the details and I will send Sean."

Just outside of Gaza, was a garage housing several military vehicles. Rabbit and Jumper led the way. For security reasons, they were only going by their call signs(names).

Sean, Big John, stayed in back of them to cover them. They were all flying under the enemy's radar, but someone had visually spotted them. Now flack was all around them. Both Israeli jets dropped their smart bombs and turned away. The ammunition in the garage soon made a large explosion and they knew that they had hit their target. Rabbit took a lucky hit and was not going far. She turned towards the sea and then ejected.

Her F-35 was lost and her carriage was heading towards the water. She hit hard and everything went black. In the fall, her hand struck the canopy hard and she fractured her wrist.

"Jumper, I'll fly down and pick up our Rabbit."

"Big John, how're you going to do that?"

"Trust me, Jumper." Sean lowered his F-40 to the cockpit and lowered his tailgate. Using a wench, he raised Rabbit out of her carriage and onto a seat. He strapped her in and took off Rabbit's helmet to find a beautiful, Diane Gilbert. She was breathing, but unconscious. With a grappling hook, he picked up her bag. Next, he radioed Jumper that she was alive and safe. Next, he notified Mossad that Rabbit had gone down and he had her. "I recommend taking her back to my doctor in Utah."

After checking in with the PM, Mossad replied, "The PM said you have a go on that." Sean then pushed the Home button and his bird shot up into the outer atmosphere and home to Utah.

Captain Diane Gilbert had been hit by a lucky round and lost her engine. With no place to land, she was instructed to eject. Sean saw her eject and turned to recover her. With the permission of the PM, Sean had Dr. Best check her out. When Sean indicated her gender, Dr. Best decided to bring an RN, Rachel Morales.

Diane had hit the water hard and broke her wrist. Yes, the house had a small Xray unit. Rachel Morales undressed the pilot and put her in a night shirt. The wrist required a brace and that was applied. Rachel would stay at Sean's guest home while the pilot remained under sedation. The Utah ranch had two homes and the ladies occupied the second one.

The world watched as Israel used the utmost restraint. PM Gandle didn't respond with his emotions. He guided his military with precision. Hamas lost a Headquarters building and anything close to it, but Gaza was not bombed.

Egypt decided that the boarder there needed to become a small lake to raise fish. That should take care of the tunneling.

CMN reported that Hamas had admitted to using 5,000 rockets in attacking the Israeli cities.

Diane woke up wearing a night gown. Diane's broken wrist had a brace on it and the pain was not easing. Diane started to get out of bed, but she noticed the catheter. Just then, Rachel walked in to check on her patient.

"Let me take that out for you." Rachel didn't wait for permission. She just walked up and removed it.

"Hey, that hurt! Who are you and where am I?"

"You are on General Shannon's ranch, in Utah. His son Sean brought you here, three days ago. "It's now the 25th of June, 2021.

"Are you my doctor?"

"No. I work with Dr. Best. He examined you and put the brace on your wrist."

"What's wrong with my wrist?"

"You've broken a couple of small bones there."

"And how do you know that? Someone here have Xray vision?"

Diane was getting a little fisty, but Rachel didn't respond in kind.

"No. General Shannon has a small Xray machine."

"So, you're used to treating people here, on the ranch?"

"I think you need to speak with Sean." Rachel didn't know how much to reveal to Diane so she left.

Diane hopped out of bed and started to follow her, but a strong desire to pee made her turn and head towards the restroom. After she finished her business, she walked into the living room. There sat one handsome young man. Rachel noticed the pause for what it was and filed it away.

Sean stood up and introduced himself. "Hi. I'm Sean Shannon."

Realizing she was only wearing a night shirt, Diane just nodded. "Why am I here?"

"You crashed and I sat down my aircraft and put you on board. It seemed logical to me since I had you, to bring you to the ranch and have our Dr. Best check you out. You were not conscious."

"You were flying an F-35. They don't just sit down!" Diane didn't like being lied to. Now she was getting angry.

"Rachel will give you some different clothes to put on and then I'll show you my aircraft." With that, Rachel motioned for Diane to follow her and the ladies left.

President Terry Jones woke up tired, again. He had Covid, again. So he wouldn't be leaving the White House. But, the world didn't stop because he was sick. The VP could handle most of the meetings, but he was still the President of the most powerful nation in the world. His economy was the largest and his currency the most trusted. The pressure never stopped. With those thoughts, he made up his mind to not seek re-election. Also, he would stop using the nickname Teddy. It had helped him get elected, both to the Senate and the Presidency. But he would no longer be using it. Terry felt a sigh of relief.

Reality buzzed. There was a phone call from the Israeli Prime Minister. "Good morning, Mr. President."

"Stop it Josh. I'm tired. How can I help you today?"

Sean had slipped on his fish-mesh shirt and was wearing jeans. The mesh shirt worked like a girdle when he needed it. When he didn't, it was relaxed.

Diane came out wearing her flight suit. She turned down the jeans that had been offered. "Follow me."

With that, they mounted the little electric cart and drove to the hangar.

Shock was not the right word to explain Diane's expression. "What the hell is this?" Looking at the F-40. She thought she was looking at the new F-21.

Sean held a remote control in his hand and began his game. With one click, it was the F-35 with no paint on the tail. Another click and it was a British F-35. Another click and it was a Cessna. Still another click and it was a Bell chopper. One more click and it was an F-40.

Diane stood there with her mouth open, but with nothing coming out. Sean explained, "They were all holograms."

"How is that possible?"

"Would you like to go for another ride?"

"I don't remember the first one. Is this the new F-21?"

Sharon Alexander and Frank were at the Pentagon getting used to their new digs. PM Gandle called on Frank's cell to thank Frank for his help. Because Sharon was there, Frank put it on speaker. Sharon jumped in, "Mr. Prime Minister, we don't know what you are talking about, but you are welcome." Everyone just laughed.

After the call and Sharon's departure, Frank sat down in his chair. He had been nominated for his fourth star. He would be the new leader of the U S military. He had been nominated to become the Chief of the Joint Chiefs. Congress had to approve of his new position and rank, but it was a done deal.

Sipping his coffee, he thought about how life works. In March of 2020, he had ejected from his F-22. He had been the squadron commander of the 27th there at Joint Base Langley. Soon, he would have pinned on full colonel, 0-6. There in the hospital, they were talking about unplugging the injured pilot. He wasn't waking up from his coma. Sara divorced him and took their son, Sean, with her to her family in Albany, New York. The Air Force gave up on Frank as well. They medically retired him at the rank of full colonel. He would be receiving a retirement from the Air Force as well as a medical retirement, at least until they unplugged him and let him die.

Beek had stepped in and inserted the medicine his brain needed to relax and heal. Kelly was his next of kin and was preparing to have him transferred to a rehab center. Except, Frank woke up.

Frank had lost both legs because of his accident. His broken arm had healed, but he was still needing help getting back into his old life. The answer was Sergeant Leroy Brown. Leroy needed to drive him around and help get him settled back into his home. Once a rising star in the Air Force, Frank's career was over, finished. Beek was needing to find a home for his three aircraft from the planet Zuppo. Frank had always been the right answer, but now it would be easier to release the aircraft to him. Now, he was totally free.

Beek had been set to return home, except for the cancer diagnosis. Now he would be staying on earth for as long as he lived. Frank had gone with him for the surgery and stayed to help Beek out. Beek's replacement had arrived and was ready to assume command. Except on Zuppo, a commander is commander until he is not. That meant that Adam was still the commander (the Beek) as long as he was on earth. Beek's replacement was number two, until Adam died.

The new Beek wanted the company and the aircraft. He got neither. Frank's sons, Kelly and Sean, moved the Starfires to Hangar 51 in Nevada. They had both been given scholarships but it was no longer possible to use them. Sharon placed them on active duty within the Air Force as Second Lieutenants. They were assigned to Homeland Security and reported only to their father, Frank.

The new Beek, Julius, was not giving up his quest of creating an empire. He needed the aircraft and the company, but he would make do without them. Western Sahara would be his starting point and then he would have moved across the northern part of Africa. Adam put a stop to those plans with four rounds from Frank's 9-mil. Julius dropped dead there in front of Adam. Julius's plans were then carried forward by his generals. Without air support, those attempts failed, also. Those involved then fled to Algeria. The Berbers melted back into the desert.

President Jones had pinned the Congressional Medal of Honor on Frank in June of that year. The Secretary of the Air Force liked Frank's fire. She brought him back onto active duty and made him her aide. Along with the job came two stars. A year later, a third star was to be added on. Except now, he was waiting for news on a fourth. Sharon Alexander wasn't waiting for the official word. She had Frank pin on his fourth. These events reminded everyone of General Haig's quick advancement. Now, Frank was wearing four stars as well.

Several of the 5,000 rockets fired landed and blew up things. Some of the rockets were intercepted by the Israeli defense dome. There were more than a thousand deaths with many more being treated at local hospitals. Hamas had spread out it's targets so no one hospital was overwhelmed.

Diane just stood there looking at this strange aircraft. "We are calling this an F-40, Starfire. It's more sophisticated than either the F-21, F-22, or F-35. The Air Force doesn't have any of these."

"What are you telling me?"

"These three birds belong to my father."

"No way!"

"I can't tell you the details."

"Or won't!"

"Okay. If I tell you the details, you won't believe me."

"Liar."

"My father has three of these. The Air Force wouldn't give me one of these to fly. I'm too young."

"I agree with that. These aircraft belong to the Chief of the Joint Chiefs?"

"That's right. His company made them."

"Sure and not the Air Force?"

"Right. Let's fly and after we land, I'll tell you a story you won't believe." The electric cart was very light, but Sean left it on the side of the F-40. With the ramp lowered, they walked on, into the Starfire. Both put on their helmets and hooked up their oxygen. Sean punched a few keys on the instrument panel and #3 fired up. It taxied out to the runway and lifted off. Sean had punched in Orbit, so that's where they went. Sean's shirt tightened and he looked over at a very distressed Diane.

After three minutes of afterburner thrust, the Starfire leveled off and began to orbit the earth. "Okay. Now we need to go back down because I need to pee." What had been higher was now about to come out.

"There's a toilet right in front of you. Just grab the hose and do your business."

"You've got to be kidding me?" She used the hose and looked over at Sean to see his reaction.

"Now, push the blue button and choose from the Meals Ready To Eat." Sean pushed his blue button and selected a coke and a breakfast sandwich.

Just shaking her head, Diane followed suit. She chose to drink apple juice along with her breakfast sandwich. "I didn't know that the F-21 was this far along in development."

"Again, this is not the new F-21. We are calling it the F-40 Starfire. It's been around for seventy years."

"No way, Jose!"

"When we get down, I'll tell you the story."

Ahkeem was angry with the Prime Minister. Why hadn't he come out swinging?

President Jones was very happy that Josh had not unleashed his power on the stupid little leader of Hamas. When the time was right, he would back a Palestinian State. But, not with stupid leaders like Ahkeem.

David Dodd stopped by his office in DC and picked up a few things. Movers would take care of the rest of the stuff. His staff had a job, but he was leaving the senate to take charge of the Zuppo company. The governor would appoint another person to fill out the rest of his term. David was turning one hundred, but looked like he was approaching his sixties. Officially, he was the new Beek. Anything dealing with his planet would need to go thru him.

After one orbit around the planet, Sean pushed the home button. #3 dove and Diane squealed as they dropped down to Utah. The back hatch came open and they both bounced on off the F-40. At the front door of his home, Diane grabbed Sean and kissed him hard.

Sean liked it.

Rachel opened the door on the kiss. Rachel took in Sean's reaction to the kiss, as well as Diane's. Whispering to Diane, "Put your claws back in Cougar. I'm leaving, but don't be hitting on this guy. Got it?"

Diane liked Sean's response, but not Rachel's.

"Tell me your story."

Sean liked the attention he was getting from this beautiful lady. "Okay, but at first you won't believe it."

Tea was offered and accepted. Now, relaxing in the living room, Diane was ready for Sean's Story.

"In 1949, a spaceship and some people from the planet Zuppo came to earth for a visit."

"Okay. You were right. I don't believe you."

"Shut up and just listen. Their leader was called Beek. It was a commander's rank from their planet. All of the people chose American sounding names. Beek chose Adam Green. On Zuppo, he had worked as an aerospace engineer. He helped to develop the F-40, Starfire."

"Life was still settling down from WWII. Korea would fight and get settled. Along the way, Adam started an Aerospace corporation for consulting. He would call it Zuppo."

"Also along the way, a race for space hit the fast track. Russia and the Soviet Union launched their efforts. Yuri Gagarin was a Soviet Cosmonaut and the first person to leave earth's atmosphere.

We had been working on an aircraft that could reach outer space. We would call it the Blackbird, SR-71. Adam's company played a major role in its development. Remember, this happened in the 50's. From this effort, we developed space suits. President Kennedy told NASA to shake a leg and beat Russia to the moon. We did. After that, Zuppo would become a common name in aerospace engineering consulting."

"Advance up to now. It was now time for Adam to retire and return to Zuppo. Last year, Adam's replacement arrived, Julius, and Adam was supposed to go back to Zuppo. But, we found out Adam had stage-4 cancer. It's a two-year trip back and he would not have survived it. So, he stayed here. Again, but before he retired, he turned over three F-40s to my father to use as he saw fit to fight against wrong, like a vigilante."

"So, I just saw one more in the hangar."

"That's bird number 2 and Kelly flies it."

"Where's the third?"

"I fly this one and dad has another one in a hangar near DC."

"No way! The Air Force has three F-40s?"

"These belong to my father and not the Air Force. The Secretary of Defense knows about the aircraft and their locations."

"Come on. Not in DC?"

"Can you say hologram? Our father was teaching us about the F-40, but now he's really busy with US military stuff."

Rachel needed to interrupt. "Excuse me. Sean, can you show me where Adam is buried?"

"Sure. He's out here next to our barn."

"Mom's coming by to see it. This will be her first visit. Sean, you should know that Adam was my father. My mother, Ann, stayed here to be with her man."

"What? Adam told us he didn't have a family."

"That's the way it had to be."

"After her visit, I'll be returning to the city."

Diane heard all of the conversation, but she couldn't believe it. You're telling me you are here from Zuppo?"

"Yes and no. I've never been there, but my parents are from there. I'm from Utah, laugh out loud."

Diane returned to her room to freshen-up and use the restroom. There on her nightstand was a note she hadn't seen before.

You're fine.

I'm next door. Sean

There with it were her phone and Id. When she came back out, she had some questions for Sean. "So, who's instructing you now on flying the F-40?"

"For the last few weeks, no one. Let's go and visit Adam." So they all got on the electric cart for a trip to Adam's grave.

President Jones was tired of being tired. The new elections couldn't come soon enough. "Sharon, congress has approved Frank's promotion. He is officially a general now."

"Thank you, Mr. President. I'll let him know."

Frank got a call from PM Gandle. "Hello Frank."

"Hello Mr. Prime Minister."

"Please, just call me Joshua. I now know the location of where the rockets were made. They were Iranian, but made in Syria."

"Can you fax me that information? I'm in DC. Just send it to my home computer."

"We will do it. Frank, you can't do everything. I recommend you use my Mossad pilot, Captain Gilbert, to fly your third aircraft."

"Let me think some on that. Bye for now."

Adam Shannon's tombstone read: Arrived September 2, 1949 and Departed June 2, 2021. Rachel was now in tears. She placed her hand on his stone and told Adam good-bye. Next, she knelt down and cried. She would never see her father alive, again. Rachel stayed on her knees for a good twenty minutes.

Ann Morales arrived later in the day. She and Rachel made the trip to the grave alone. Then, they returned to the city.

Speaking to Diane, Sean suggested that they go out. "Let's go over to Rollie's café and get supper."

"You just saved my life. How can I possibly refuse?"

"It's not really a date. We just need to get away from here for a little bit. I also thought you might like to know more about the F-40."

"I think you're stalling to give yourself more time to make up more of this BS."

"No. You can't make up a better story."

"Okay. I'll go, just because you saved my life, but don't try for sex later." Both laughed.

Later at the café, PM Gandle phoned Sean, "How are you doing my young Mr. Shannon?"

"I'm good Sir. How can I help you?"

"I'm calling you so that you know it's really me. I have an assignment for Captain Gilbert. I'm going to want her to stay there in Utah for a while and fly the third F-40. Your father has agreed to it. He's got his hands full for right now. If you're okay with instructing Captain Gilbert on what you know about the F-40, then she'll be staying for a while."

"Holy cow! Sure. You know I've still got a lot to learn."

"Diane is probably going crazy wondering who and what you are talking about. Pass the phone over to her."

Diane's eyes were saying What? "Hello."

"Hello Diane. This is Joshua Gandle."

"Yes Sir. What can I do for you?"

"I need you to stay in Utah for the time being. I've permission for you to fly the third F-40."

"Sir, Sean is telling me that these birds belong to his father. Can that be?"

"Beek and I had been friends for a long time. He was set to go back to Zuppo and wanted to leave the F-40s with a good and trustworthy friend. I recommended Frank Shannon. He turned the aircraft over to Frank and then he found out he had stage-4 cancer. So Frank was left in charge of the birds and the ranch. David Dodd is heading up the company, Zuppo, for now. Also, Senator Dodd is the new Beek. You can trust the wild stories from Sean."

"Sir, my clothes and stuff."

"I think you and the young Shannon can take care of all of that. Good night."

"Good night and thanks."

The next day, Diane and Sean made a trip to Jerusalem in the F-40 and Diane's lessons began. All she needed were her clothes. The second house was fully furnished.

The F-40 was unlike anything she had ever flown. The afterburner thrust on top of the magnetic field reversal. The Gs were doubled. The fish-mesh shirt helped, but it was not something that she would be getting used to, soon. There were no peddles on the floor. Things to grip and hold onto were connected to the seats. Everything was laid out on the dash/consol. It was not difficult to learn. It was just different.

"Tell me about Beek."

"Okay. Beek was his rank and not his name. He chose Adam Green for a name. He arrived here on earth on September 2, 1949, at the age of 42. He had been working as an aerospace engineer. Adam helped design the F-40 and then was asked by his government to bring some people to earth. It's a two-year trip. Some of the time they slept and some of the time they were awake. When they arrived, they all chose American English names and did more schooling in English. They learned about our history and what had just finished, WWII."

"Soon, Adam started a consulting company, Zuppo, named after his planet. Adam brought his ideas to our government about a high speed aircraft that could go to the edge of our atmosphere. We don't have the same metals here that they used in constructing the F-40, so that combination of metals had to get figured out. The plane would become the SR-71, Blackbird. It flew so fast that the air acted like sandpaper. The paint had to be incorporated into the metal. The F-40 is faster. The SR-71 could orbit the earth. The SR-71's pilots wore spacesuits. In the race for space, we gained ground."

"President Kennedy told NASA to hurry up and beat Russia and the Soviets to the moon. Then he got them the money they needed and we put a man on the moon first."

In December of 2021, Kelly graduated from Georgetown University. Kelly had finished in three and a half years. During that span, Frank had crashed. Kelly had become a Lieutenant in the Air Force. And now he was graduating. Graduation was a great thing, but for Kelly things were kind of tense. His Mom and Dad both came along with Sean and a Captain Gilbert. Kelly's parents hadn't spoken since his mother had divorced his dad. Sean stayed close to Frank but had greeted his mother. Sara had hugged her son and then left. The celebrating was done with his wife, Jax, dad, Sean, and Diane. Kelly and Jax would visit with his mom back at the Holiday Inn.

Now Kelly could focus more on just flying. His dad had an assignment for him and his brother. They were to blow up a hangar in Syria, near Damascus.

Diane had agreed to join the group of vigilantes. She now lived in the second house. Diane would be Sean's co-pilot. Diane had her own fishnet shirt and some lessons on the F-40. She would go on the mission, but only helping Sean.

For now, General Frank Shannon would be staying in the background. PM Gandle had faxed him the details of the location of the rocket factory. Frank in turn passed this information on to his new team. The Vigilante team had grown. It still included Chief Brown in the DC area, but it had added two airmen for the Ranch. The airmen lived at Dugway and worked ten hours every other day.

The Onaqui Security Service, a small private security service, set up a guard at the entrance to the ranch. You could no longer just drive onto the ranch. A gate was set up at the only entrance to the ranch. If you had a gate opener, you could enter whenever. Without the electric gate opener, a guard was there from seven A.M. until ten P.M. Two miles of a 7-foot-tall fence was set up with another mile at each end going perpendicular. The Shannon Ranch was adjacent to the reservation for the Onaqui Mountain herd of wild horses. This new fence would not separate the horses from their watering holes.

After a return to the hangar, all three boarded number 2. The two airmen loaded four smart bombs onto the aircraft.

Kelly fired up number 2 and it headed into orbit, using the plain F-35 hologram. Kelly had the "Con." Sean was his Co. Diane was there to learn more. Once over Israel, Kelly lowered his aircraft to refuel. He used his NATO Code and refueled. Next, Sean punched in the new coordinates and they flew to the rocket factory area. Sean pushed the release button and 4 smart bombs took out one rocket factory. The video showed a large explosion and the new team returned to orbit and then to Utah. Kelly kept his aircraft, but dropped off his passengers. For now, Kelly was still living in the DC area home with his father and wife, Jax.

Once again at the door, Diane planted a hard kiss onto Sean. Without Rachel to stop the two, they continued into his bedroom.

As the new year rolled in, Frank had worries over Russia's movements along the Ukraine border. To the Secretary of Defense, "Would it be okay with you if we had the SR-71 check out Russia's border with Ukraine?"

"Sure Frank. Go for it."

With that permission, he contacted the Chief of the Air Force, General Jackson, "Hello Demark. I need a favor. Can you deploy an SR-71 to take some photos of the Russian-Ukraine boarder? I'd like to know how much it has changed?"

"As you command, Boss."

"Just Frank."

"Whatever you say, Boss."

The report from the Blackbird was that more troops were close to the Ukrainian border. With the Secretary of Defense, Frank went and reported this news to President Jones. Photos are worth a thousand words.

President Jones was saddened by the photos. War was coming. How much war was coming. "I'll give Putin a call, but I don't expect the truth from him."

With that, he picked up the red phone and called Russia. "Good morning Mr. President."

"And good morning to you as well. How can I help you today?"

"You can tell me you are not going to invade Ukraine."

"Yes, we are not going to invade Ukraine. We are just strengthening our borders. That Zelensky is a sneaky fellow. Have a good day."

With that, both parties hung up. "So he's going to invade Ukraine soon. Sharon, get our military on alert. No long term leaves. We won't change our Defcon just yet."

"Yes, Mr. President." With that Sharon and Frank had things to do back at the Pentagon, so they left.

In 2014, Russia had annexed the Crimea, now called the Republic of Krym. Ukraine had done nothing except cry over the annexation. The Crimea had for a long time been the retirement home for many VIP Russians. So, no one there fussed. The locals had made a lot of money building homes for those well to do Russian retirees.

A comedian by the name of Zelensky was tired of all that Russia was doing to his country. His politicians were afraid of Russia. He was not. He ran for the President's position and was elected.

Olena and Volodymyr Zelensky were holding onto each other. They didn't know when or if they would hold onto each other again. "I need you to leave with the kids within the hour. Peter has said Putin is coming. I believe he will try to take us out and replace us with more of his people. I'll need you to take the Volkswagen. Oleg will go with you to help you get settled. I trust him with my life and I am trusting him with you and the kids. Don't tell anyone you are leaving forever and don't tell anyone your location. Just as I have Peter talking with me, Putin will have his helpers. We don't know who they might be, so say nothing. Turn off your phone until you call me tonight. I don't want them tracking your signal. I love you."

No more words were exchanged. Tearfully Olena left her husband, maybe for the last time. She and Oleg left to gather her bags and two kids.

Next, Zelensky met with his political staff. Half of the staff would go with Radionov, his Vice President, and Smirnov, his Prime Minister, and half would stay in Kiev with him.

"I will not tell you how I know, but I know that Putin will invade Ukraine in the coming days. We need to spread out now. I will be staying here with a few of you. I want everyone else safe. Go where you will but don't tell anyone. Putin will have people you trust reporting back to him."

"Andrew (Andrew Koshkin, Minister of Defense), I want every rifle ready for use. When we know where he is attacking, I'll want every adult male to have one. All others will need to evacuate. Thousands of Ukrainians will die, and millions will leave their homes. Let's not be caught unprepared."

"Sir, where will you be?"

"Moving. I'll be moving so he can't find me."

For this time, his people staying with him were just a few:

Andrew Koshkin – defense

Victoria Abramova (female) – finance

General Boris Ershov – Chief of military

General Kapustin Stas – his deputy

Major Sergei Medvedev – commander of the special forces guarding the group

Sean and Diane flew together every day. Fuel wasn't a problem because the aircraft compressed nature's air for fuel. Jet fuel was just used when they used full thrust after-burners. There had been a lot of movement along the Ukrainian boarder. Russian troops were edging closer to Ukraine on a daily basis. Kelly and Sean sent their photos over to Mossad who then sent them to the CIA who then shared them with Ukraine. Ukraine was using its own drones and was not surprised by the photos. NATO would not enter Ukraine and give Putin a reason to come on in. Putin would just have to enter on his own.

Today, February 24th, 2022, Putin's army crossed the border. Thousands of troops and a few hundred tanks along with big artillery guns. Putin hoped the fighting would last only weeks. His Yes Men were telling him that Ukraine would crumble quickly.

Putin wanted Kiev within days. He needed to replace the Zelensky family with his own puppet. Then, he would become an invited guest. A special forces squad of 24 assassins landed in the capital to find and kill President Zelensky, his wife, and two kids. Then everything else would fall into place.

General Ershov got a call that it was happening. Ukrainian drones captured the Russian movement, but artillery was also booming away.

Zelensky's team went into hiding. The first place was a cave within the city. Zelensky didn't use any of his government's buildings. Instead, he had his special forces units hide there and wait to be attacked.

Those females with autos began moving west. Others took the trains as room allowed. In the east, one of the artillery targets was the train station. Hundreds died before their trains could pull out.

At twenty miles out of the city center for Kiev, artillery began blasting. Russian troops were shooting at anything that moved. Tanks were blasting anything that looked like a threat. Aircraft were bombing factories. Apartment buildings were a primary target. Hospitals and schools were not safe.

In the center of the city of Kiev, the assassins landed in choppers. The leadership only brought 24, but they were the best. The first stop was Zelensky's residence. There, they found Ukrainian special forces and a battle. With no progress, they simply blew up the residence.

Next, the 20 left, heading over to other government buildings. Once there, they found more Ukrainian special forces. These buildings were also blown. After three days of searching, the Russians were down to a dozen. They kept following their possibilities. After a week, they were down to five. They called in one chopper to evacuate them.

The Russians troops had been told that NATO was occupying Ukraine and preparing to enter Russia. Except as the troops entered, they didn't find any NATO troops, just Ukrainians and most of them civilians. Still, homes and apartment buildings were blown. Those males out and about were killed whether they carried weapons or not. Some women also lost their lives. Some soldiers were involved in crimes like rape.

In Mariupol, the resistance lasted longer. The steel mill had been a good place to hide. Soldiers and civilians fled there. Eventually, that too fell.

Still, Putin was not a happy man. Some of his yes men found themselves on house arrest. The capitulation of Ukraine didn't happen. The Kiev area was vacated by Russian troops with a few parting artillery shots. As the Russian troops pulled back, they looted and took autos that had keys.

Now Odessa was attacked, but the Ukrainians were not passive here. Some Russian vessels found the bottom of the Black Sea. Then Ukraine began shipping out its grain harvest. Turkey said, "Come on out."

President Zelensky went on national TV and spoke to anyone listening. "We did not invite Russia to come into our country. We will not bow down to the Tzar Putin. We will fight him. Can you help us?"

Frank got permission to fly two of his birds to Romania and the NATO base at Constanta. From there, the new vigilante team flew missions into Ukraine. When the Russians retreated from Kiev, some of their equipment was blown. Tanks were exploded. Artillery was also hit by what seemed to be Mig-26s.

Two F-40s were stationed at Constanta, Romania with the third staying in the DC hangar. The first few trips into Ukraine, all three rode in one of the F-40s. After a couple of trips, Sean and Diane split from Kelly and acted as his wingman. Diane knew about flying, but she wasn't ready to fly an F-40 alone. Also, she liked her co-pilot.

NATO had not been together on sanctions at first, but they were beginning to see a problem with Russia and Ukraine. It seemed that Russia was also looking at Moldova. The separatists in Transnistria were interested in support and recognition from Russia.

Belarus had been supporting Russia's efforts in Ukraine until its population said it needed to stop. Thousands of Belarus civilians marched in protest against Russia's invasion of Ukraine. Belarus would not be sending any troops to help Russia in Ukraine.

Germany had held out for a long time. They didn't know how they could make it thru the winter months without Russian oil. Finally, they agreed on the sanctions.

Russia wanted support from China, but the US was spending a lot of money in China's factories and that money would stop if China supported Russia in any way.

President Jones knew that Russia would not stop with Ukraine. He released one billion in credit to Zelensky. Other NATO countries added equipment and some offered to train their military on the use of their weapons. The vigilante team took out at least a hundred Russian tanks. Choppers were not safe to fly. Ground to air missiles were shooting them down. Even some Migs were lost. Still, Russia had far superior weaponry. But, Ukraine was fighting.

Some of the earlier cities taken by Russian troops had been re-taken by Ukrainians fighting for their homes. Thousands of Ukrainians had died in the early fighting. Another ten million Ukrainians had left their homes. Europeans were welcoming those who feared for their lives.

Meeting with President Jones in his office, the Secretary of Defense and General Shannon updated him. Sharon speaking, "Mr. President, Mossad is estimating that Russia has lost more than five hundred tanks, more than five hundred personnel carriers, more than two hundred choppers and over twenty-five thousand soldiers."

"Frank, let's bring your team back for a time. They deserve some R & R."

"Yes Sir."

In September, Putin activated his two million reserves. Also, he activated the draft. He would draft 300,000 lucky Russian citizens. Putin was running out of time. His country and supporters would only take so much. Putin had not been able to bring in any good mercenaries. The ones that had come only ran away in the heat of battle. Now, raw civilians would be brought into uniform and sent into a heated war zone. With that good news, maybe two million Russian males headed towards its borders.

The vigilante team made one more foray into Ukraine before leaving. They blew up the bridge connecting Russia and the Crimea. Supplies would have to find another route. And for one final blow, they bombed the Russian base at Novofedorivka. Then buttons for home were pushed and the F-40s shot up into orbit and home. For Kelly, home was in the DC area. Sean and Diane headed to Utah and the Shannon ranch. #3 parked itself in the hangar and a tired team rode the cart over to their homes. Frank had kept some Jack in the cupboard. Two Jack and cokes and then some sleep.

For Kelly, Jax met him at the DC hangar. They just held onto each other and both cried. Tensions were released as both were together again. Jax drove them home and Kelly had a martini and fell into bed. Sex would have to wait a few hours, but it would happen. For right now, they just needed to hold each other and sleep.

Protests were now mounting to Putin's actions, so he fled to his retreat. Once there, he met with the head of his defense, General Peter Maslov.

"Sir, we have lost one hundred thousand troops."

"So, you are not doing your job. You are relieved."

"So, I'm telling you how it's going and you fire me?"

"You've had the best equipment and well trained men and you are not doing your job."

"Sir, you can't easily win against people protecting their homeland."

"It is not their homeland any longer. I annexed it."

"Sir, those are only words."

"Good-bye General."

With that, General Peter Maslov was escorted to a chopper waiting to take him back to Moscow. Putin had become a Tzar. His daughter would not replace him. He would pick from his small group of supporters. For now, martial law put him in total control of Russia.

One of those supporting him was General Evgeniy Isakov. He received his new promotion on October 12, 2022. His orders were to take it to Zelensky.

This time fifty special forces soldiers were sent to Kiev to hunt him down. Two choppers were needed to carry them into Kiev. The first place they looked was the cave. But, Zelensky and his staff had moved to their second hiding place, the Library. Special Ukrainian forces met with the assassin squad with weapons blazing. After a short battle, the cave was blown.

President Jones met with Frank and Sharon. "I think your people have helped quite a bit in Ukraine, Frank. Let's keep them home for other jobs. Zelensky can use all of the weapons he has to work his way back."

"Yes Sir. I'll pass that along to the team."

"I haven't heard any more from our friend, Beek. How's he doing?"

"Sir, the cancer took him back in June. He appointed Senator Dodd to replace him. So, he's the new Beek. I'll have him give you his contact information."

"What about the one man from Zuppo that came to be the new Beek?"

Smiling, Sharon responded. "Adam didn't like him so he fired him. I don't know where he and his co-workers ended up. Adam appointed David Dodd to be the new Beek."

Zelensky hadn't seen Olena or the kids since the Russian invasion began. It would have to stay that way for a while. His country was getting the weapons needed to retake what had been stolen. All of Europe was behind him and he was fighting for them. If NATO entered his country, Russia would be free to use nuclear weapons to defend itself. So, NATO would only supply weapons. Ukraine was bleeding, but so was the Russian military.

CMN was reporting that mass graves had been found in the cities retaken by the Ukrainian troops.

The British Prime Minister told the world that Russia and Putin were criminals.

Kelly enjoyed his time off with his wife. They kept his aircraft in the DC hangar along with Frank's. Sean and Diane were only flying #3.

Russia was still in Syria as were American troops. Here, they were friends and did not fire at each other. The Space Station was also still working well.

Frank speaking with Sean in the DC home, "Hello."

"That's not a normal Hello."

"It's time for Diane to go solo."

"You want us to break up?"

"I want Diane to make her Solo flight."

"Oh, wow. I was thinking about the two of us."

"Let her take Sara back to her squadron at Nevatim. She needs to spend some time with her family. That means she'll have time to think about you and beyond. It'll give you time to think about your future, as well."

"I know. I like her being around."

Frank wanted to tell Diane. "Is it okay if I tell her?"

With that, Diane Gilbert flew #1 back to Israel. The Mossad had prepared a hangar for her to use along with a special security guard. Diane's family had spoken with her by video phone, but had not been with her in person for more than a year. Diane's father was Isaac from the New York City area. Her mom, Ruth, was from Jerusalem but had attended New York City University. Isaac had been a teacher there and fell in love with Ruth.

Flying is a standard kind of thing. Diane had flown the T-6 and then the T-38. At the end of that time, she made a solo flight from Mississippi to California. Then she went on to F-16 flight school for another eight months and then back to Nevatim Airbase, Israel. There, she pinned on captain. Mossad was interested in her and her classmate, Adam Sultani. They would join up with Mossad and enter F-35 training. Her solo flight with her F-35 was from Texas to Nevatim, delivering a new F-35.

Once again, her solo flight with the F-40 was to Nevatim Airbase. As she arrived, she turned off the hologram. People saw the F-40 for the first time. Captain Sultani saw what had picked her up out of the water. He was happy for her and her aircraft. She showed all of the holograms and they laughed together. Diane would have to take him for a ride later. Right now, she needed to go home and be with her family.

Sean took his bird to Albany for a visit with Mom, Sara. He wanted to just relax. His time with Diane had been good, but stressful. Now, time with Mom was just relaxing. Sean was able to park his bird at the Reserve Base there at Albany. The base commander was his first visitor. Sean was wearing his Air Force flight suit with his name and rank. Colonel Hopkins was an active Reserve officer working full-time as the base's commander.

"This is an amazing looking bird Sean. I'll need a ride later."

"Small price to pay for parking it here. Sure Sir."

Sara now had her own place and Sean could really relax without entertaining grandparents or cousins. Once again, some Jack and coke and a bed. He would sleep for almost two days. Then his family demanded their time with him.

War is a terrible thing. Hamas had launched more than 5,000 rockets into Israel. Thousands of civilians had been killed or injured.

PM Gandle came onto CMN and told, "If you claim to be Hamas, then you are dead. We will hunt you down and kill you for what you have done. People in Northern Gaza, prepare for fire. Hamas, we are coming for you."

Located in his office beneath the hospital, Akheem smiled and laughed right before the fire from the explosion entered his office. The subway was filled with fire.

Terry was thinking about being "The President." He decided that he needed to use all of his influence with the Prime Minister of Israel to stop the war. He would promise him anything. Then he called. "Good evening, Joshua."

"Mr. President. Tell me what's on your mind, as if I didn't already know."

"How can I get a ninety-day ceasefire?"

"Get Hamas to release the other one hundred hostages."

"Okay. I'll get on it." With that, Terry smiled and called in his staff.

Prime Minister Gandle called for Captains Sultani and Gilbert. "The Mossad needs good leadership and you have done a great job. Today, I want to promote both of you to Major. Diane, this would mean you return to us and give back the F-40."

Major Medvedev had been waiting for Putin's special forces to attack, but today that changed. He ordered his soldiers to wipe out the invaders, to the man. President Zelensky had moved for the last time. It took only three days for his troops to wipe out the invaders. President Zelensky went on TV and announced where he was and invited Putin to try and kill him one more time. In Moscow, Putin was furious. One more commander would get fired.

Iran ordered twenty drones to attack Israel. None of the twenty made it into Israel. Jordan took out all of them. The king announced, "You don't have permission to fly over us and endanger my people." The world was surprised. Iran was surprised.

Terry Jones called in the Secretary of Defense. "Sharon, as quietly as you can, I want you to send the Navy CBs into Gaza. I want to clean up the rubble. The United Nations workers need shelter and protection. Let's set up some mobile camps." (The Naval Construction Battalion, Seabees)

Days turned into weeks and Sean re-entered the University of Utah in Salt Lake City. His classes were only on MWF schedule. All of his credits from the Air Force Academy transferred.

Kelly was glad to be home. His wife, Jax, was still a fulltime student. For now, his flying was just in the DC area.

Sean's heart was breaking, but he was not going to contact Diane. He would wait for her to contact him. She was an amazing person, but Maybe not his. He cried as he thought those words, Maybe not his.

Kelly flew Diane back to Nevatim. She was silent the whole time. Diane was wearing her Israeli uniform with her new rank. When she got out of the F-40 no words were spoken. Diane walked away from a life that had made her the happiest that she had ever been. Tears rolled down her face as she wondered why she was walking away from the happiest she had ever been. It wasn't the sex. It was the Sean.

Sean was in the school library working on his research paper. It's hard to read with tears in your eyes. So, he gave up and left the library. If love makes you feel like this then I don't want to love again.

Then, one day in the library, Sean looked across the room and there sat Diane. In a slow motion, he moved to get closer to this person that looked like Diane. It couldn't be his Diane. She lived in Israel.

As he sat down across from her, he just looked at her.

"I'm sorry Sean. I couldn't stay away."

Sean ran around the table and kissed her and held the love of his life. No words were spoken. They just held each other. After a bit, they left the library. A few classmates actually clapped as they left the library.

Sean asked Diane, "Now what?"

"Sean, that's up to you."

"No, you are a Major in the Mossad."

"No, I'm a civilian holding my former boyfriend."

"Can we just go home?"

With that, they went back to the ranch, turning in her rental along the way.

www.ingramcontent.com/pod-product-compliance
Lightning Source LLC
Chambersburg PA
CBHW050457110726
47899CB00003B/982